THERE'S A SHARK AT MY SCHOOL

SHARON J BOYCE
SUZANNE HOUGHTON

This is Seymour, he lives in my pool.
He's cheeky and sneaky and totally cool.

I'm ready for school and my shoes have been found,
when a tap on the window makes me turn 'round.

'Hi Annie,' says Seymour,
waving his fin
and flashing his teeth
in a big cheeky grin.

'Okay, I think that's a brilliant idea,
but do what I say. Is that perfectly clear?'

He thinks for a moment, then gives a sly wink.
'Of course! I'll be faultless, what else would you think?'

Finding my wagon, I squeeze Seymour in.
'That tickles,' he laughs as I tuck in his fin.

I cover him up,
so he'll be a surprise,
leaving a gap
for his nose and his eyes.

On the way I get questions from all sorts of folk.
'What have you got there?'
'Do you mind if I poke?'

When I get to the classroom, my friends try to guess,
but they all get it wrong, so I say with finesse...

Whispers and stares make me feel like a star.
I throw back the tarp with a flourish.

'TA DAH!'

'His name is Seymour, he's my favourite pet.'
Miss Bright is trembling and dripping with sweat.

The class is in chaos, there's kids everywhere.
My friends all cheer loudly. Miss Bright's on her chair.

'I'm hungry,' says Seymour and flops on the floor
and wiggles and flips all the way out the door.

The canteen is mayhem, the staff shake like jelly.
Seymour looks pleased with his big, fat round belly.

'Bad Shark!' I say. 'Did you eat the fish fingers?'
'Not me, I'd never!' But a fishy smell lingers...

'I'll get the wagon. You'd better stay here.'
But Seymour comes up with a clever idea...

The next time I see him he's building with sand,
a six-storey castle that's really quite grand.

Water from hoses, bubblers and taps
fills up the moat but it runs out the gaps.

It floods from the sandpit, gushing through doors, soaking the classrooms, hallways and floors.

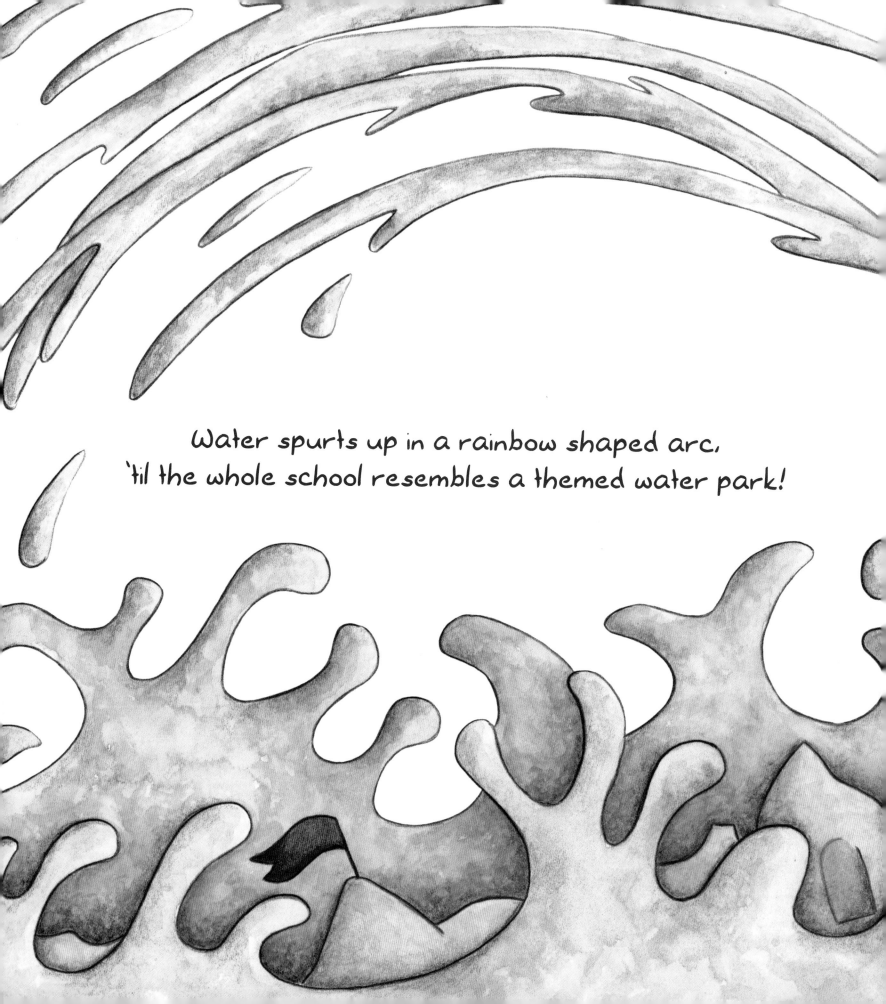

Water spurts up in a rainbow shaped arc,
'til the whole school resembles a themed water park!

splashing in puddles

and dancing through spray.

We slosh 'round the oval and play games of tag.
Seymour's the fastest at getting the flag.

'That shark needs to go!' hollers Principal Mac.
'In case you were wondering, he's not welcome back!'

Seymour and I float around in my pool,
sipping on lemonade, icy and cool.

'I don't think school's the right place for a shark.'
'No,' chuckles Seymour. 'Let's go to the park!'